My Roots
Roger
Billy
James
Roy
Herford
Joey
Jr.
Terry
Joe Roach

# ROOTS

BY

JOE ROACH

Cadmus Publishing
CadmusPublishing.com

# ROOTS

 Published by Cadmus Publishing LLC. P. O. Box 8664. Haledon, NJ 07538

Web: Cadmuspublishing.com
Web: Booksbyprisoners.com
Web: MusicbyPrisoners.com
Facebook.com/Cadmuspublishing
Business email: admin@cadmuspublishing.com
Phone: 360.565.6459

ISBN# 978-1-63751-524-2

Book Catalog Info Categories:

Cadmus Publishing
CadmusPublishing.com

# Chapter 1 My Roots

I remember back in the early seventies when I was just a boy. It was miserable—muggy and hot. No wind blew to stir the heat, making it even worse. If the wind had blown just a little, it would've made a big difference, especially in the summertime!

We were dirt-road poor, having to go to bed with the chickens because there was no electricity, no water, no plumbing in the little shack where I was born. This is where life's blessings began. What we thought were struggles back then, looking back fifty-four years later, were really blessings.

Some of us seem to forget the dirt road we came from. Most of my family that remembers has passed away. Thirty years ago, we didn't even have a cemetery. Now, the cemetery is overflowing with headstones.

# ROOTS BY JOE ROACH

What I remember about growing up was never looked at for what it really was—love and blessings. Nowadays, if you don't have running water, electricity, or plumbing, it's considered abuse and neglect.

Back then, you got plenty of rest. When the sun went down, you went to bed. Why stay up just to sit in the dark? "And blow out them candles," Dad would say.

After a long night's rest, it was always nice to wake up early to the smell of homemade buttermilk biscuits, fried eggs from a black skillet, bacon, and gravy made from the bacon grease.

All of this was cooked on a wood stove at around 5:00 a.m. before daylight. Mom cooked every morning, six days a week. Daddy would sit at the table with a lantern hanging over it while he ate. Outside, we could hear the old 1949 pulpwood truck running, warming up. Most of the time, it was already loaded from the day before. He had to haul that load to the pulpwood yard, unload it, and stack it in a boxcar. That's what he woke up to every day—except Sunday. Daddy never believed in working on Sundays. He said anytime he ever tried, it ended up costing him more than he made.

Me and my brother Jay were the only two born at the time to witness those hard times. That old shack that sits inside the cow field as you enter Roach Town—the one with the porch falling in—that's where me and my brother Jay were born. That's where our journey began.

I was only eleven months younger than Jay. I've been on his heels ever since I took my first steps. He's my real and true best friend and brother. I miss him every day. When I think back to where we came from, I'm fifty-four years old now, but the love I have planted in my heart for my older brother Jay still makes my eyes water.

Sure, we were dirt-road poor—but we didn't know, and we didn't care. We had each other. That's all that mattered to us back then.

As soon as we were big enough to use the outhouse on our own, we were with Dad on his logging job. Our older cousins, Ricky and Ronnie Roach, worked for Dad and helped keep us safe. That's how me and my brother were raised.

When we were no more than four and five years old, Mom and Dad raised tobacco on the backside of Uncle Dave's farm. It was maybe four miles around the main road to Dave's on Dundee Road.

Before Dad left for work, he'd harness the big work mule so that when daylight came, Mom could load me and my brother on its back. She'd walk that mule to the field, where she'd plow what she could of the twenty-acre field before dark. Then, she'd unhook the plow, load us back onto the mule, and walk it all the way back to Roach Town, where we lived in that little two-room shack.

That's where our roots were planted—at the end of that dirt road. That's where we started learning about life and everything else we needed to know about what we once thought were struggles, but now see as blessings.

Don't try to tell us about hard times. I'm sure we could tell you a thing or two about what we call blessings.

Now, if you ask someone what a rain tree is, they think you're making it up. A rain tree is what was used to hook a plow, a slide, or an attachment behind a mule or horse to pull with.

Back then, everything was done by hand. Pulpwood was loaded by hand. Logs were rolled onto the truck using skid poles and can hooks. Not many people knew what a can hook was. Most never did to begin with. But a can hook saved a lot of backaches. Way back then, if you didn't have one, you knew it by the end of a log-turning day at the sawmill.

Me and my brother Jay knew what all these things were by the time we were five years old. So when Dad said, "Get the rain tree to hook behind the mule to drag logs with," or "Hook it to the plow to plow the garden, the cornfield, or the tobacco field," we knew exactly what he was talking about.

Same with the can hook. When he sent me or my brother to get it, we knew what he meant. We came back with a can hook.

If you came back with something crazy instead, trust me, that didn't happen but once.

Nowadays, people just laugh when you don't know something. Back then, you got blessed with an ass-whooping.

The next time he sent you for a can hook, you came back with a can hook.

Nothing pissed Daddy off more than us not paying attention. He should've never had to show us what a rain tree or a can hook was in the first place—not the way me and my brother were raised. Act dumb if you want—you'll find a boot in your ass.

We learned. We didn't forget.

People like my Dad, my uncles, my Grandpa June, and my Uncle Dave Roach—they helped teach me. They made sure I knew what mattered.

# Chapter 2

I have two brothers—Jay, he's the oldest, and Jeremy, he's the baby. He don't like when I call him the baby. I don't do it 'cause he's the youngest—I do it 'cause he's my baby brother, and I love him.

Nothing will ever change that. I can't stop the love I have for my baby brother. No matter how he feels about me, it don't change the love in my heart for him.

My brother Jay—I know I pissed him off plenty. He's been there for me when people wanted to act like I had nobody. He's stuck his neck out for me more times than I can count—more times than he should've.

He's done a lot for me throughout our life, and he never owed me nothing. He was just being the brother he's always been since we were kids—when I was that little boy following behind him every step of the way.

# ROOTS BY JOE ROACH

I remember waking up on a blanket on the floor of the little shack. Me and my brother slept wherever we laid down—couch, chair, floor—it didn't matter. When I woke up, beside me, I'd find my brother. Two boys who fell asleep without a bath. I love it!

I know Jay wants to kick my ass right now—sorry, brother. We was both raised dirt-road poor. Don't act like you don't know—'cause trust me, you do.

Mama said when we were little, my brother fell asleep with a bottle in his mouth. While he was sleeping, rats were stealing milk from what leaked out, running down his jaw to his ear. The rats even ate part of his ear. Don't go looking at his ear now—I told you this, he's already pissed off at me!

Just seeing him every morning brought a smile across my face. You never know real love until you stop and look back at what love really was. We never had to say it—we saw it and felt it every day.

One thing about love—you may forget, but love will never forget you.

## ROOTS BY JOE ROACH

We abandon love before it abandons us.

The same way we've done God so many times.

I just wanted my brother—and the whole world—to know how much I love my brothers.

I'm loyal and true to my roots, no matter how many mistakes I make. It ain't my family's fault I turned out this way. My family has always, and still does, help me however they can. My roots are planted solid.

But my mind—it wanders off and gets lost a lot. Then I find myself in trouble.

It's been this way most my life. I'm pretty used to it now.

Growing up, I never saw the inside of a church. Daddy was the only God I knew back then.

Daddy's hands across my back, my butt, my head—they felt as hard as steel.

But in my heart, they were as soft as cotton.

To know what kind of man my Daddy is, you'd have to read Job from the Bible. That's the easiest way to explain what a wonderful, great person my Daddy was—and still is. Not just to me, but to everyone in the Roach family.

He's been more dedicated to the Roach family than anyone else I know.

Daddy never cared about his own wants or needs. I'm not even sure he ever took the time to. He was too busy trying to help and be good to everyone else.

Daddy cared just as much for Larry and Jason as he did for any of us. Our love was always a brother's love. They were raised next door to us in Roach Town. Chubby, their dad, cared about us the same way Dad cared about his two boys.

Chubby's two boys were the only ones Daddy took to like that. He cared a lot for Larry and Jason.

## ROOTS BY JOE ROACH

Dad and his brothers built Roach Town.

Each one started out in that little shack.

If that old shack could talk, what a story it would tell.

The roots of Roach Town started there.

That shack now looks like it needs pushing over. The new generation don't care about the roots and memories that shack represents—the life of the Roach family.

That shack was the beginning of Roach Mountain. My uncle Roy said as long as he was alive, it would stand until it rotted to the ground.

You'd think, with more than forty of us being born and raised in Roach Town, our mamas would've been the ones that kept the kids together.

But it was Daddy and my uncles' love that built Roach Town.

## ROOTS BY JOE ROACH

Our mamas birthed us.

But our Daddy built us—and kept us together.

Mama was a great mama. But only God is greater than our Daddy.

When I was a boy growing up, in my eyes, Daddy was the only God I knew.

My Daddy and uncles called Roach Town God's country when I was a kid.

Now, it looks like an abandoned ghost town.

It's sad to look around and see the ones who built us are now only remembered by memories and headstones.

Dad and my Uncle Johnny are the only two brothers left.

Roach Town looks like an abandoned place with no love.

## ROOTS BY JOE ROACH

That's what happens when kids grow up not caring about their roots.

Ashamed to let people know they had to use a Johnny house growing up.

Ashamed they had to take a bath in a wash pan or a round metal tub.

Sometimes, when it didn't rain for weeks, the same tub of water would be used all week.

By the time it was poured out, it looked like mop water.

This is the life I remember.

The life others don't want people to know we lived.

I'm proud to talk about my family's roots.

The ones worth talking about.

Look around at how far they've come.

Then you'll see how dedicated my Daddy and uncles were—to make sure their kids had a better life than they did.

They never cared about themselves.

They only cared about us growing up.

These were the real men.

The ones it took to plant the roots they planted—roots they hoped would stand for generations to come.

Life is much more beautiful when people care more for others than for themselves.

The new generation now—it's hard to say they much different than the people that love them.

# Chapter 3

Nothing in life ever stays the same. Playing fair ain't even a rule anymore!

The logging industry is growing bigger than ever.

I was reading an article in an old magazine I found in the prison library about storms and damaged timber salvage. In 2021, Southeast Louisiana lost around 5.0 million tons of pine and about 68 million tons of hardwood due to hurricane damage. That’s an estimated 200,000 acres—over $300 million lost.

We ain’t never had to experience that much being destroyed from a storm here in Virginia—not that I can remember in my lifetime. That was some serious storm damage.

It seems like the more timber they cut here in Virginia, the worse the storms get all across the state.

Before, when storms came in from the coast, the mountains and trees knocked them back, turning them into the kind of storms we were used to having. But with hundreds of thousands of acres being cleared, that open space is fueling the storms' strength like never before.

Look at Claytor Lake—2024.

Rarely do you see storms that powerful in the heart of western Virginia. But now, so much timber is being cut that it's making it possible for storms to build up power and tear through multiple states.

Before, we didn't really have to worry about storms like we do now.

Larry, Jason, and Jay—if I had to guess, they're probably pushing out at least a thousand loads a week. That's a lot of timber being cut. And if I had to guess, 90% of that is either clear-cutting or pine thinning.

There are so many ways to harvest timber—select cut, clear cut, pine thinning.

Nichols Logging in Huddleston is another big timber harvester. They're wonderful people, and they're top-of-the-line loggers. I've always thought a lot of Bobby and his son, Bo.

The Roach family has always spoken highly of them, and we all know the struggles every logger faces at some point in life.

I can say this—Bobby Nichols is another great, hardworking man, along with his son, Bobby Jr. I know for a fact they're dedicated to their roots.

Wonderful people.

Daddy started JTR Logging when me and my brother were younger. He always made sure we both had the same opportunities to be a part of JTR Logging when we got older.

My brother stuck with my daddy, helping build JTR Logging into the successful company it is today.

With help from other dedicated family members, like my Uncle Hertford—he was a great man. He got killed while working for JTR Logging.

Then there's Rex Krantz, our first cousin—he's been dedicated to my daddy and brother for over thirty years now.

And he's still going strong.

That's what you do when you come from strong roots.

Jerry T. Roach—that's my dad. He's been good to everybody.

And those who were dedicated to helping build JTR Logging—Dad always made sure they were blessed in return.

That's the kind of man my dad has always been.

Larry and Jason helped build JTR Logging, too.

Now Larry—I'd say he's probably one of the biggest timber harvesters in Virginia.

He's come a long way from that dead-end dirt road we were all born and raised on.

He's been blessed—and because of that, he's helped bless others in the Roach family.

He also helps others step up their game when it comes to logging in Virginia.

Jason—he's doing great for himself.

His wife, Jessica—I think she's one of the most respected women I've ever known.

You probably won't hear me say that about another woman except for my sister, Jody.

Jessica—Jason's wife—she's just a wonderful, kindhearted person.

# ROOTS BY JOE ROACH

A great mama.

A great wife to Jason.

Her and Jason together—they're a great team.

I'd like to say—keep it up.

The world could use more people like Jason and Jessica Roach.

The Roach family has a lot of great people in it.

I've only met a couple in our family who wouldn't give you the shirt off their back.

Thirty years ago, the old king of our family was our uncle.

He was a great man—but he made sure none of us ate from the table he ate from.

That's how he secured his kingdom for generations.

Now Larry is the king—but he does things differently.

If there ain't a chair for you at his table, he'll get up and give you his.

That's why he's blessed.

Him and my brother Jay—they both the same way.

Back to JTR Logging—throughout the '90s, I wasn't around much.

I was in prison—took a whole different path than my brother.

I started serving my first ten years in the late '90s.

While I was in prison, JTR Logging grew.

Through the late '90s, early 2000s, my brother and dad stepped up the heat to build JTR Logging.

With the help they had—Hertford, Rex, Larry, and Jason—it would've been hard to stop a real and true Roach family.

These guys were raised with the help of Papa Roach.

That's what they called him—Kingpin Papa Roach.

Daddy started out with mules, farm tractors, cable skidders, and an old Homelite chainsaw.

He built JTR Logging from the ground up—with determination, dedication, and a whole lot of back-breaking hard work.

Jerry T. Roach Jr.—that's my brother.

He's the one responsible for transitioning JTR Logging from back-breaking manual labor to fully mechanized operations around the year 2000.

By 2007, Daddy retired—finally able to do what he always wished he could do.

He wanted to retire and be a farmer.

And he got his wish.

That business transition—that was my brother's decision.

And that decision was made with the dedicated people he and Dad had helping build JTR Logging.

# Chapter 4

This is what keeps JTR Logging proud and how Jay operates his business today.

I'm sure God's proud of the way my brother cares more for others than himself and his business.

He got that from Papa Roach, and I'm sure God will continue to bless him for being the person he is to everyone—along with Larry, Jason, Jeremy, Wesley, and so many more loggers we know.

My brother said something I'll never forget—something I hope to live by when I start my business again, if ever possible.

This is how he wants people to know JTR Logging:

JTR Logging is not about JTR Logging.

It's about the lumber companies, foresters, and landowners he harvests timber for.

He looks at it like it's a privilege to be chosen to harvest certain tracts of timber.

He said when he hears some loggers talk, it sounds like they forget who works for who.

The success of JTR Logging has always come from the respect his employees show—because that represents his company.

None of the success would have ever been possible without the timber providers to begin with.

So JTR Logging will forever be humble to all of its timber providers—no matter who they are.

His company is always dedicated to them.

He said when timber providers open the door for JTR Logging to harvest their timber, he wants them to be able to close that door proudly when he's done—knowing they chose the right team to harvest their timber.

He said the respectful members of JTR Logging—the ones who have been dedicated to helping him build his logging business—have done a great and wonderful job with the utmost respect for everyone they deal with, always honest and professional.

That alone, he feels, is what's gotten him this far—and if it's God's will, this will be the way it continues.

He wakes up feeling blessed every day.

Their success will always depend on their effort, safety, and performance in every harvest.

And this—this is what he relies on his workers to do professionally.

This is how he wants his company to look at every day's success:

Working for you, not JTR Logging.

Because God blessed him through you, not JTR Logging.

I remember conversations I've had with a lot of good people—people I've met either when I was logging for myself, sitting around with my brothers Jay & Jeremy, Larry & Jason, and many others.

I'm blessed to know so many good people I've met throughout this journey called life's blessings.

I know my family has to be some of the best—and biggest—timber harvesters in Virginia.

And I'm proud of that.

# Chapter 5

In 2007, Daddy retired and turned the business over to my brother. At the same time, Larry & Jason were out on their own, building Larry's logging company—Pro Logging.

Pro Logging and JTR Logging have stuck together the whole way.

My brother, being the owner of JTR Logging, bought a used Morbark chipper in 2007.

Larry stepped up and got himself and Jason a new Morbark chipper.

By 2015, my brother bought a new Bandit chipper.

They both kept building—my brother built Southern Logging, another successful logging business, plus helped others build many more.

Larry kept going full throttle—and he's still going strong today.

By now, he's built at least ten successful logging businesses that I know of—along with developing a trucking company big enough to keep his logging operations running smoothly.

Not only that—he helps other logging businesses when they need help getting their product from point A to point B.

Larry has helped a lot of people.

If anybody says anything other than Jay & Larry are great people, they gotta have serious issues going on in their life.

Larry & Jay helped me get my own logging business started.

They both like seeing me do good. They told me that the people who matter were actually proud of how I was doing.

They didn't care about the money.

They were just happy that I was doing well for myself.

People don't know blessings until it's too late.

Larry got where he is through dedication and determination.

Another person I'd like to mention—someone I've always thought highly of—is Dewey.

He's someone I've always considered a friend.

We had some fun times hanging out when we were younger.

He's seen struggles in his life, too.

He also works for Larry and has his own trucking company.

Just wanted to say—I heard Dewey was doing good.

I'm glad to say you are my friend, Dewey.

You're a great person.

After a lot of help from my family, when I started logging, I hauled my logs to Wendell Cox.

He's another person who has always helped me—like I was his own kid.

Everyone knows how I feel about my Daddy.

But the only other person I feel about like my Daddy is Wendell Cox.

Since I was a boy, Wendell has always been like my second Daddy.

Wendell has helped me through life more than I can ever say.

I'm thankful to be a part of the lives of people like Wendell, Jay, Larry, Jason, Dewey, Jeremy, Wesley, Johnny, Dad, Leroy, Clayton, Bobby, Bo, Russell, Big Paul, Butch, Clyde.

Facts is—I know all these great and wonderful people.

These are the kinds of people that built Huddleston and the Smith Mountain Lake area into the beautiful place it is today.

As long as I have friends like this, God will bless me.

God is a great and wonderful God.

God has surely continued to bless me—and all the great people I know.

I hope to continue having this outlook on life.

# Chapter 6

Being curious, I decided to read the Bible—that was around three years ago.

That's why I speak of so many blessings.

Even though I didn't know God back then, He blessed me when I didn't even know what blessings were.

He still blessed me—through so many people.

Through my brother, my Daddy, Larry, Wendell, Toby, and many more.

I could go on and on.

I never looked at all the things my family and others did for me as the blessings they really were.

Looking back now—nobody in my family owed me anything.

If anything, I owe them more than I could ever make right in a lifetime.

The most important things in life are:

✓ Family

✓ Health

✓ Friends

And above all—God.

God is the most real friend we will ever have—besides family.

I started reading about God a few years ago because I needed to find peace in my heart.

That's when I decided to read the Bible—

No church group.

Just me—one-on-one with God.

I learned about faith, prayer, and hope—things everybody needs in this world.

## ROOTS BY JOE ROACH

If you got faith in God, you will receive many blessings.

Through Jesus is the only way to our Father in the Kingdom of Heaven.

Through Jesus is the only way to receive the gift of Eternal Life.

Eternal Life has no starting point.

And it has no ending point.

It's for eternity.

I read the Bible.

Then I tried to understand the Bible.

Then I started learning about God.

I don't go to church—I do my reading, studying, and learning about God by myself.

God says as long as we have faith in Him, that's what He cares about.

# Chapter 7

God says as long as we believe in Him and trust Him, we will always be blessed. I believe that.

I was watching a movie about the Bible on Christmas Day. Some people say Jesus was set up and betrayed. He wasn't. That was part of God's plan—to prove to people the cruelty and wickedness in their hearts. These kinds of people would kill Jesus the first chance they got. And just as He knew they would—they did.

God created the world. Then He created Adam. Then Eve—to live a life in Paradise.

But Adam failed to keep Eve in check. She snuck off with the Devil, took a bite of the apple— and there went paradise.

Now, here we are in a beautiful world, but full of cruel and wicked people. This time, people are strung out on drugs, and they will destroy anything in their path to support their addiction.

Before God sent Jesus, we were living in hell. Jesus died to change all that—to give us eternal life. He showed us unconditional love and gave us the strength to live, survive, and bring love back into this world.

Learning about God, I find peace and love through my relationship with Him—through reading the Bible. God will never abandon us—that's a promise from God. I've learned this by reading the Bible, and I know it's a promise that will never be broken.

I do know we cannot find peace without God. We will continue to be frustrated until we have God in our lives. God only asks us to believe and trust in Him—and He will do the rest.

You hear about people's good intentions—but that's how we ended up in trouble to begin with. Good intentions don't always lead to good results. Even I have good intentions.

It was a blessing for me to start reading the Bible. Nobody needs God in their life more than I do. He couldn't have chosen a better time. He's helped me see that I'm not a bad person—I just needed a little faith. And that—He could help me with. Like He has helped me over the past three years since I started reading the Bible.

I count my blessings daily because every day is a blessing. Every day is another day closer to being with God. And one day, I'll be reunited with my son, JJ. That's the day I'll truly be blessed.

# Chapter 8

I enjoy talking about my family's accomplishments—how they've built a strong, successful life through hard work and dedication.

I remember back when I was doing well for myself—I had my own small logging business.

Larry Roach—a great person— had top-of-the-line, state-of-the-art TigerCat equipment.

He owned and operated one of the largest and most experienced logging operations—Pro Logging.

He's been professionally operating for over twenty years.

If you ask me—Larry is the largest timber harvester in Virginia.

Every goal he set—he successfully accomplished.

That comes from dedication.

My brother Jay has slowed down a lot since our mama's brother—our uncle Hertford—was killed on the job.

That took a lot out of him.

Because our uncle was more than just our uncle—he was our brother.

Mama and Daddy raised Hertford along with me and my brother Jay when we were little.

There was a lot of love in our home at all times.

You never heard the words "I love you" because you could see it and feel it all around you.

Actions always spoke louder than words.

After our uncle's death, Jay started watching his machine operators closely— making sure everyone operated with caution and safety.

He said, “Not every skitter operator is skilled to operate on any ground. Operating big equipment can get you hurt—even killed.”

So on each track, he decides who’s the best operator for that terrain—to get the job done safely.

Most of Jay’s employees are family.

They’ve operated pretty much every piece of equipment on the job.

But still—a lot of times, Jay would rather risk his own life on a mountainside than let another family member do it.

We have one cousin that’s been with Jay for so long— they can read each other’s minds.

That’s Rex Krantz.

He’s been by my brother’s side the whole way.

Rex is one of the biggest pieces of the puzzle when it comes to JTR Logging.

Whoever could make the ground speed and do the job safely— that was Rex.

Trust me.

My brother Jay depends on Rex.

He's reliable, dependable, and dedicated to JTR Logging.

He is the most dedicated and reliable worker JTR Logging has had—now going on thirty years.

He will never be able to be replaced.

The same went for Hertford.

Hertford will forever be missed and never forgotten.

Jay started his second business—Southern Logging.

Southern Logging focused mainly on select cutting, private-owned tracks, and mountain tracks.

Mountain tracks take time—so Jay liked being able to leave Rex in charge of JTR Logging while he harvested the select-cut tracks.

The select-cut tracks were manually cut with chainsaws— a lot of dozer road work and cabling.

It had to be nice timber—if not, it wasn't worth it.

JTR Logging had to continue its daily operations.

JTR Logging was designed for production— they couldn't afford downtime.

JTR Logging had to be operating at full throttle.

JTR Logging was a business built from success, goals, and daily accomplishments.

Jay Roach is highly experienced when it comes to any kind of logging— Whether it's flatland or cliffside logging— He's all about caution and safety.

Cliffside may take longer, but he wants everyone alive when the job is done.

One thing I can say about Jay, Larry, Jason, and Jeremy— They are what real family is supposed to be.

Real.

At the end of every day.

# Chapter 9

I really enjoy talking about my family—how great they are and how successful they've been. Even though I'm not a part of the Roach family logging business, I'm proud to say that Jay, Larry, Jason, and Jeremy are my family.

Jay and Larry helped me, along with other great people. I messed that up. I can say Jay and Larry, and all the others, bent over backward to help me when others were hoping they wouldn't give me the time of day.

The whole time they were helping me, certain ones were already putting a knife in my back. Not everyone in the Roach family is about helping each other the way Jay and Larry are about helping family.

Some of the others are quick to accept but have no intention of offering anything in return. The reason Jay and Larry have done so well is because they bless others before blessing themselves. God is proud of that. I'm not sure what kind of relationship they have with God, but whatever it is, they're surely doing things right. For two people to do so well, God has to be pleased with what they are doing.

Larry and Jason had a great dad, plus they had our daddy, who cared a lot for them. Larry and Jason cared a lot for Mom and Dad, and Mom and Dad cared for them just like they were their own. I've always cared for both of them the same as my brothers.

Jason works for his own logging and trucking company now—Red Line Trucking. Jason Roach has been dedicated to the Roach family since he was old enough to sit on a piece of equipment. He's another one who's been successful at building and helping build many logging businesses. He's never set a goal he didn't accomplish.

His accomplishments are big—there's never been a time he didn't lend a hand to anyone he could help better themselves in the logging industry. He didn't hesitate. He's a one-of-a-kind hard worker, and his dedication and loyalty make him the wonderful and great person he is.

I've never seen anyone operate a Morbark chipper the way he can. He's never been one to have downtime. He keeps every piece of equipment well-maintained to have as little downtime as possible.

His trucks are even better maintained than the equipment—if that's even possible. He makes sure all his drivers keep the necessary replacement parts on hand for immediate repairs.

He also makes sure his drivers keep plenty of bulbs, light lenses, and reflector tape on hand at all times.

Jason is all about safety—when it comes to his employees, everyone on the job, and while his trucks are on state highways.

He, along with Jay, Jeremy, Wesley, Larry, and other professional truck owners, believe that using reflector tape cuts the chances of an accident by more than 75%, especially when hauling at night.

They all keep their logging and chip trailers heavily coated with reflector tape, making them highly visible at night.

When motorists pass any of Jason's trucks, they are in safe hands. He thanks all motorists for their respect, and they have his utmost respect. That's how he likes to operate all his trucks on Virginia highways.

If there's ever a complaint about one of his drivers, do not hesitate to contact Jason Roach at Red Line Trucking.

That goes for any business the Roach family owns or operates.

The Roach family is dedicated to all motorists, their well-being, and their safety.

Jeremy Roach—Hard Timz LLC—is another dedicated logger who owns his own trucking company. He also runs one of Larry's crews.

I was riding down Red House Road when I saw a landing being cleared for a logging company to set up. It was off the road, and I couldn't tell whose equipment it was.

That was around eight o'clock in the morning. I was headed to look at a small piece of standing timber on Red House Road.

When I came back through around one o'clock that afternoon, two trucks were pulling onto the main road in a curve. I slowed down as I eased up to the flagman directing traffic.

I asked the guy, "Hey, buddy, who's cutting the timber?"

He said, "Jeremy Roach—Hard Timz LLC."

Hell, that's my brother.

So I turned in and drove down to the landing, where I saw my brother. It was a surprise because I hadn't seen him in a while.

I knew he worked for Larry running a crew, but I never thought he was doing it this big. The reason I didn't know was because I had been living in Roanoke.

I pretty much stayed on that end, doing select cutting and mountainside tracks for Leroy Hurt. Roanoke is a good ways from Red House Road in Gladys, VA.

When I pulled up, we shook hands and hugged. Our soft hearts made both of our eyes water.

I looked around at all the nice equipment—all TigerCat. I said to Jeremy, "So this is how you're doing it now?"

"Yep, this is how we're doing it," he said.

When Larry transitioned his jobs over to TigerCat equipment, that's when he helped me get my start. He had a lot of used equipment—Caterpillar, Barko, TimberJack, Hydro-Ax, John Deere—he had a big selection.

After seeing Jeremy's job and how it operated with all TigerCat equipment, I can see why Larry had so much used equipment parked.

You know the saying—nothing runs like a John Deere?

Well, you don't really get blessed until you run TigerCat equipment.

TigerCat has blessed so many people. Some would rather go to their job on Sunday than go to church.

Never will you hear or see blessings like this from any other brand of machine than TigerCat.

I can say this because it didn't take me but a minute to figure out why Larry helped me with his used equipment.

To me, then and now, even though it wasn't TigerCat, it was still a blessing to me.

# Chapter 10

The more I watch Jeremy and his crew operate with state-of-the-art TigerCat equipment, the more I understand how Dad must have felt when he went from dragging logs with a mule to using a farm tractor, an old homemade buggy, and then a winch tractor.

Back then, that was a blessing. It's no different now—the only way to be blessed in this business is through TigerCat equipment.

I asked Jeremy to tell me more about TigerCat, and I've never seen anyone put out loads every ten minutes. They had to have a drop deck to swap trailers because hot loading—trying to load trucks as they arrived—was impossible. The trucks just couldn't keep up.

TigerCat's reputation is for no downtime or very little, if any. Jeremy said he wouldn't have anything on his job other than TigerCat equipment.

He told me, “I can load twenty-five loads starting at nine in the morning, and by two o’clock, I’m heading home to spend time with my family.”

When you buy TigerCat equipment, you’re not just buying top-of-the-line, state-of-the-art machinery—you’re buying time. Time you can use to spend with your family.

Jeremy has two beautiful children, and he loves kids, so anytime he can, he’s spending it with those babies.

Time is something you can’t buy anywhere. But it comes free with TigerCat equipment.

I feel like it’s safe to say—after watching my family’s struggles and seeing the blessings that have come from using TigerCat—TigerCat has to be the godfather of all equipment!

Time is more valuable than anything else.

Life insurance companies should be thankful for TigerCat for the lives they save. The stress-free operation of these machines probably adds ten more years to a logger's life. Anyone running TigerCat equipment is never late on their payments. Most of them pay off their homes and businesses in half the time.

If you stop and think about what I'm saying—based on watching my family's struggles over the years—you'll understand.

I watched my daddy and uncles humble themselves, working with mules, then farm tractors, then cable skidders. They felt blessed back then, despite every struggle. But back then, you never even heard of TigerCat. Men worked themselves into early graves. The ones who weren't killed by the dangers of logging often died from being worn down before they reached sixty.

My uncle Billy died in his fifties, worked and stressed into an early grave. My uncle Roger went the same way. My uncle Roy died in his early sixties, worked and stressed to death. He was hauled in by horse and buggy when he was laid to rest.

James was the baby boy of the Roach brothers. He died in his sixties—that was Larry and Jason's dad.

Lyn was killed by a tree in his twenties. My uncle Hertford was killed on my brother's job in his forties. My cousin Terry was killed on my logging job in his forties.

Scotty was killed in a car accident. My son was killed in a car accident at twenty years old. My cousin Danny died in his thirties, maybe forties.

The Roach family is fading away. What used to be the town that built us now looks like a ghost town.

I just wanted to say—I wish we could have had more time with all the ones we've lost.

If we had back then what we have today, I think most of them would still be alive.

So when I say, “When you buy TigerCat, you’re buying time to spend with family, friends, and loved ones,” I believe that’s the truest statement ever said.

That’s all facts.

No one can challenge that statement.

So don’t wait another day—contact Larry Roach at Pro Logging. He can and will help you buy more time with your family by selling you state-of-the-art, top-of-the-line TigerCat equipment.

His businesses are based in Altavista, VA. Along with logging, he sells TigerCat equipment.

# Chapter 11

Jeremy had a 625H TigerCat six-wheeler skidder. I thought that was a huge machine until I saw the 635H pull into the loading deck. Now that was massive. The grapple was even more impressive.

But when I saw what it was pulling behind it, I said to myself, "That's crazy!"

Three skids with the 635H filled a chip trailer with chips. Two skids with the 635H loaded a trailer with tree-length pine.

Within an hour, Jeremy loaded more trailers than I could load all day.

The 234 TigerCat knuckle boom loader—Jeremy says he would highly recommend it for production loggers. It handles great and doesn't bounce like so many other machines he's been on before.

He claims the hydraulic system is much more powerful, the buck saw reacts instantly on command, and the delimber has more pressure on its knives.

Jeremy said TigerCat is the only reason he's logging today.

That's another powerful statement. That should tell you—success comes first when it comes to TigerCat equipment.

The 2016 TigerCat 855D track cutter is another fine machine. I've been around a lot of equipment, and this cutter is one of the most desirable machines I've seen.

It's especially good for slopes and hillsides.

For ground speed, a good cutter would be the 724E rubber tire cutter from TigerCat. Some say the 720G is even better. I've heard nothing but good things about both machines.

Another nice machine is the 620E TigerCat skidder—a highly desirable machine.

One thing I know about TigerCat machines—if you show them even a little love, they'll continue to bless you.

TigerCat is a tough machine.

If you're a logger and feel like you haven't been blessed, that's because you don't operate with TigerCat equipment.

When you go to Larry's jobs, everywhere you look—state-of-the-art TigerCat equipment.

Come to my job, and you'll think you've stepped into Jurassic Park. My equipment looks as old as dinosaurs.

I still feel blessed.

# Chapter 12

I remember so much about me and my brother back when we were growing up. We'd sneak out of the house, hide in the floorboard of his old pulpwood truck, and cover up with a blanket like he wouldn't see us—just so we could miss school and go with him to the woods to work.

Dad was a great man, and seeing how bad we wanted to go with him, he let us miss school that day.

He started letting us miss every Friday unless it was raining, then we'd miss Monday. Dad was always loyal to his word. He never told us something and then let us down. I love my daddy more than life itself.

Me being only eleven months younger than Jay, he never really got a break—unless I went to stay with my Uncle Chubby over the summer. Chubby was Larry and Jason's dad. They weren't born at the time, but Chubby cut pulpwood just like all his brothers.

Chubby lived in Sycamore then. He hadn't moved to Roach Town yet. He lived across the tracks, up on the hill, in a trailer beside his Aunt Sis's house.

I remember that orange 1966 Chevy two-ton pulpwood truck. He cut and loaded that truck by himself, sometimes twice a day. These were real men—all the Roach brothers were.

I was young, maybe eight or ten years old, but I did what I could. When I heard that old Homelite chainsaw miss one time, I knew to get the gas and oil ready, because only seconds later, it would run out.

People look at me like, "Really? You poor thing." But I don't feel that way at all.

The whole time, I feel blessed to have had the great and wonderful family I did.

They taught me things most people today will never know.

If we ever had a Great Depression again, people who don't have time for me now would be blessed to know me then.

Of course, they'd say they wouldn't, because they've got money.

But money's no good when there's nothing to buy.

People nowadays don't even know how to raise a garden.

I'm not like certain people I know. I'm really not the bad person they want others to think I am. Still, I'd look out for them, because that's the heart God gave me.

A lot of the love I have to give comes from people like my daddy and my uncles. They never had to say "I love you" to anybody—you could see it and feel it every day.

All my uncles blessed me—my Grandpa and his brother, my Uncle Dave.

I liked staying with my Uncle Chubby. He liked drag racing, and every other Sunday, he'd take me with him to New London Dragstrip.

Now and then, he'd sneak me into New London Dance with him. Chubby was a hound dog!

My Uncle Johnny lived next door. He's always been good to me.

My daddy and all his brothers might be the reason I am the way I am. If anyone was spoiled, you best believe it was me.

The word "no" didn't exist for me.

I had five uncles.

When Daddy said no, I went to each one of them.

With five uncles, I never did much walking since I was old enough to see over a steering wheel.

I never had a problem asking my uncles for anything.

When they gave me something—even if Mama had told me no—Daddy said I could have it.

I swear I don't think my mama liked me much at all, with all those "I'm going to get you" looks she used to give me.

That was okay. Daddy and my uncles kept on blessing me.

"Get over it, Mama."

# Chapter 13

I remember Daddy timbering the Hancock property on Dundee Road, down by the creek.

Dad had a front-end loader, an International dozer, and a Ford Dexter winch tractor.

Me and my brother Jay were hanging onto the fenders, in and out of the woods while Dad was dragging logs.

That winch took three hands and three feet to operate.

That old tractor didn't have a cab on it.

How we stayed alive was a blessing from God—it had to be.

Back then, it was survival. Nowadays, it would be called neglect and child abuse.

To us, it's always been a blessing.

That particular day, we were hanging on to the fenders while Dad was winching.

I was holding the lock and unlock lever—up was unlock.

Dad worked the PTO lever with one hand, one foot on the clutch, the other foot on the brake.

My brother was pressing against the winch lever to keep it from kicking out.

There we were—Daddy, hanging onto the steering wheel, the front wheels of the tractor in the air, and me and my brother struggling to hang on while working the winch at the same time.

We both knew one thing—now that tree was sliding, we better not let go of those levers, because the cussing was worse than an ass-whipping.

We'd rather get beat with a stick than disappoint our daddy.

The tree was coming…

Then, all of a sudden, the cable popped.

The front wheels slammed down so fast, my brother's foot slipped from the lever and got caught in the winch.

By the time Dad figured out what had happened, he cut the PTO off.

Jay's boot, foot, and leg had been winched into the winch.

I had the release lever.

Dad had to pull his foot and leg free.

Daddy told him to sit on the tractor seat while we fixed the cable.

Dad also had to cut the tree in half so we could skid it in two sections.

Once we got to the landing, Dad took Jay's boot off.

His foot was destroyed.

It had turned blue, veins showing, bleeding.

All the hide was gone.

Dad doused it with gas to stop the bleeding, then wrapped it with an old shirt I found in the truck seat.

With half a load already on the truck, Dad had me stay at the landing with Jay, sitting on a bucket while he finished dragging enough to fill the load.

The log truck was the only vehicle there.

Just before Dad got the last of the load, Mama pulled up and took Jay to the hospital.

That's life's real struggles.

We still look at them as blessings.

Because, at the end of that day, we were alive and together.

That's what our roots are made of—blessings and love.

Jay was out a couple of days.

While he was out, I was still hanging on to the fenders of that winch tractor.

No matter what, our roots had to grow.

A couple of days later, Jay was back—using his other foot to hold that same lever.

This was how we were born and raised.

Dirt-road poor.

Riding that mule while Mama walked it to the tobacco field to plow what she could.

These are what we call blessings.

Now can you see why God blesses us continuously?

No one can tell the real way and reasons for many blessings like I can tell about the Roach family.

Wesley Roach is a wonderful and great person. He's always thought about others before himself. You know, I think sometimes if they cared for others the way they have, they would be rich because they gave to others more than they kept for themselves.

Then again, God blesses them for the great people they are. If they were any different, they wouldn't be blessed at all. God blesses from the roots—that's where we all come from.

I just want the world to know Wesley Roach is one of a kind. A great and wonderful person. He's gone out of his way to help me, and I'm forever thankful. Maybe I'll sell a lot of copies of this book, and when and if I'm blessed to do that, I'm going to bless back those who blessed me.

If any of you know Wesley Roach, you know he's a remarkable, one-of-a-kind person. He's also dedicated to his roots. He knows where we all started—from a Johnny house, a wash pan, and a small round metal tub.

All these people I talk about, if they haven't passed away or been killed trying to survive, they know where the roots got started.

Larry, Jason, and Jeremy are the only three from the new generation that were born with old souls like we have. Their roots are planted deep.

# Chapter 14

Larry, much like his dad, has a passion for drag racing. He's on the Street Outlaws show, called "Axman." That's Larry Roach. So he's dedicated to more than just logging. He's dedicated to his family. His children are great, wonderful, and beautiful. His wife, Sarah, is a wonderful person—a beautiful wife and an awesome mother.

Russell Roach is another one I want to mention. He and his wife, Tracy, are both great people. Russell and I were logging partners at one time.

I remember when we were logging alongside the Roanoke River. Russell was operating my 230 Timberjack cable skidder. It was cold—below twenty degrees—especially down by the river. We were right on the water, and it had started icing and sleeting. We were cutting massive poplar trees, so big we had to cut each tree in sections just to get them out.

Russell was sitting right beside the river. I had run the cable about eighty feet back and hooked it to a massive poplar. My 230 had a straight 4-inch flex pipe, so it was loud. Once the tree started coming, Russell held that 353 Detroit wide open. I looked away just for a second.

All of a sudden, I heard a crazy gargling sound—then silence. The tree stopped.

The skidder was on its top. The bottom of all four skidder tires barely stuck above the water. Then, up popped Russell from beneath the river. He swam to the bank in freezing water. I helped him out and asked what happened. He said, "Hell, my guess is as good as yours. Everything was going good, then the next thing I knew, I was upside down at the bottom of the Roanoke River."

He stripped down—his clothes were frozen stiff. I had on insulated coveralls over my clothes, so I gave him my boxers and the coveralls. We started a fire to thaw him out.

By the time he got out of his clothes, they were so stiff they could stand up on their own.

Once he was warmed up, we got his Tree Farmer skidder to winch my 230 out from the Roanoke River. Only problem was, one of us had to jump back in, go under, and hook the cable around the cage of the skidder.

Guess what? I can't swim, so it wasn't me.

The temperature had dropped to near single digits. With nothing else to wear once he got wet, Russell got naked, dove in, and I tossed him the cable. He disappeared under the freezing water, then moments later, surfaced again.

I helped him onto the riverbank, where we kept the fire burning. He got dressed, and we winched my skidder from the bottom of the Roanoke River.

As for that massive poplar tree, it's still laying there, and the rest are still standing.

We counted that day as a blessing. We took our equipment and got the hell away from there. It was way too dangerous over a damn tree.

That's just one adventure me and Russell experienced together. We made a lot of money together, and I wanted the world to know he's my cousin and he means a lot to me.

He's also got a great wife, Tracy, and her sister, LaVern, and her husband. I want to give them a shoutout—two more great and wonderful people to add to my list.

LaVern, I liked her from the first time I met her. I've never disrespected her or her husband. I just wanted them to know that I consider them both dear friends and a blessing to have met.

One thing you need to know about the Roach family—whether you're my first cousin or my fifth cousin, we're cousins. Either you're my cousin or my uncle. That's just how it's always been. If your last name is Roach, that's how it goes.

Russell's daddy was Uncle Russell. Now, you want to talk about a great man? He was one of the greatest men there ever was. Nobody saw struggles like him.

Russell fell off the top of a load of logs and landed on his head. It paralyzed him from the neck down.

This makes my eyes water just writing about it, so I'll keep it simple.

Russell was someone that, if you didn't know him, you were missing out. Even after being paralyzed, his outlook on life was a blessing.

He was blessed. Those who loved him loved him a hundred times more. There will never be another man as tough and strong in mind, heart, and soul as my Uncle Russell.

I just wanted everyone to know—Russell is another one who will forever be missed and never forgotten. He was always good to me, and I'm blessed to have had him as an uncle.

I also want to mention Russell's wife, JoAnn. They surely don't make women like her anymore.

She will always be a wonderful and great person.

I've never in my life seen a woman so understanding and determined to keep her family together. She stood by Russell's side after his logging accident left him paralyzed from the neck down.

In my mind, there will never be a woman greater than JoAnn. I just wanted the whole world to know what a great person she has been—more dedicated to her family than anyone I've ever seen, never taking time for herself.

JoAnn, you are one of a kind. Not only great, but also a remarkable person.

Thank you for being the piece of the puzzle that completed it.

Your kids are great and wonderful, and I'm blessed to have you as my Aunt JoAnn.

Like I said, if your last name is Roach, you're either my uncle, my aunt, or my cousin. We all know where our roots came from.

God didn't bless just one—He blessed the whole Roach family.

You know you're a good person when you look at struggles like Russell and JoAnn faced and still say you were blessed.

You don't find people like that anymore.

FACTS.

# Chapter 15

I haven't been riding around like I used to. Most of the time, you'd find me out riding around, meeting people. That's something I've always enjoyed. Seems like most of the logging jobs in Virginia are family-related.

Where I come from, that's just how it is. The only way you get treated like family is if your last name is Roach. Loggers in Virginia were built like family. We all stick together.

I feel like there's no place like Virginia when it comes to people looking out for each other. Whether it's logging or farming, Virginia was built by great and wonderful people who stand together like family.

I remember when I was a young boy, during tobacco harvest time, all the farmers in the community would come together.

Especially back when tobacco was tied by hand onto sticks. Some were pulling while others were riding. When the men came in from their day jobs, they would hang the tobacco sticks in the barn, placing them on the tiers. Each barn had three tiers high.

During harvest season, tobacco farming and logging were the hardest jobs to do. That's pretty much what built a lot of the communities in Virginia. That's why we see each other no other way than as family.

Some people say I'm not a good person. But really, the only ones who say that are the ones starving for attention. Everybody knows me because I enjoy getting to know people. Haters have a problem with me because I know everybody.

I'm not a bad person. I want this book to help the people who don't know me but only know what they hear. Remember—don't judge a book by its cover. Don't judge a person by what you hear. There's a lot of haters in the world.

God doesn't like haters. Haters are the ones who killed Jesus.

Back when I was a kid, "hater" wasn't even a word. Back then, when you looked around, all you saw was love. Now, all you see are haters. That's how much things have changed.

Back then, people fought to stay together. Now, they fight for a reason to stay apart.

I've never seen a more forgiving family than the Roach family. Many times, I've had the ones who care about me in the family steaming mad. But still, when I got to the end of my rope, they caught me every time.

I'm sure that's part of why I still do some of the craziest things. I've been spoiled my whole life. My family is full of great and wonderful people.

I've never gone without anything I wanted because the Roach family is a big family. When one said no, I just went to the next one. I learned this when I was a boy.

Daddy wasn't the only one who whipped us where I was born and raised. If you did wrong around my uncles, they whipped you too.

I didn't mind getting whipped. Because if you whipped me like my daddy, I was going to ask you for whatever I asked my daddy for.

All my uncles were like my daddy because I stayed in trouble, and I was always blessed because I never had a problem asking for anything.

No matter what it was—when Daddy said no, one of my uncles got it for me.

That's how I was born and raised in Roach Town.

My daddy's name was Jerry, then I had all my uncles. Daddy Johnny. Daddy Roger. Daddy Billy. Daddy Chubby. Daddy Roy.

My favorite? All of them.

No other Roach kid had as many daddies as I had. That caused certain cousins to be haters.

I didn't care when I was a boy. They'd catch me away from my daddies, and they'd kick my ass. But that didn't stop me from asking their daddies for anything. I'd ask anyway. Believe me, all my uncles were good to me.

Their little haters—better known as heathens—would kick my ass a lot when I was a little boy.

Haters!

I surely miss all my uncles. If they were still alive, I'd have it made. Now that they've passed, I'm stuck here looking at haters!

I really haven't had but one kingpin hater. He passed away some months back. I've been blessed ever since.

Sad to say, but when he died, it was the greatest news I'd ever received. He made my life miserable every day. He was a kingpin hater.

Sounds cruel, but it's true—his death was a blessing to me.

Just remember, God don't like haters.

Why?

Because haters are the ones who killed Jesus.

For a hater to get to Heaven, the chances of it happening are the same as a camel getting through the eye of a needle.

That's pretty slim, if you ask me.

I don't wish that on anyone—but haters bring that on themselves. Just for being something they don't have to be—a hater!

Just because I've been blessed—don't hate on me.

Daddy said I'd see days like this when I was a young boy, going around eating from everybody else's plate, leaving them scraps. Now I see what he was talking about.

Just adding a little humor.

The ones who know me know I’ve been spoiled by the whole Roach family.

That kingpin hater? I’d go around him to all my other cousins after my uncles passed away, and I was still blessed.

Now that the kingpin hater is dead, I don’t have to sneak around anymore. I can go straight to my cousins and not have to worry about the lies made up by the kingpin hater.

I have a lot of great family.

Shane and his wife, Wanda—they have been nothing but good to me.

When my uncle Roy died, Shane continued to help me. If he could help me, he did. He gave me small tracks that were too small for him, and I helped him with bigger tracks that were mainly chips.

Shane took over his daddy's business. His daddy was my uncle Roy.

Roy helped me like I was his son.

He was my uncle, and all my uncles were good to me.

My uncle Roy was extra good to me.

He, along with Daddy, Jay, and Larry, helped me start my own business.

Shane and others helped me after my uncle Roy died.

I was no match for the kingpin hater.

The kingpin hater was taking bets at his dad's funeral on how long it would take before he took me out.

He partnered up with a certain lawman who had personal issues with me.

Within a year...

# Chapter 16

I was number three on the list of the ten most wanted people in the world.

Now, does that tell you what kind of hater he was?

He accomplished putting me out of business.

Only after the lawman he partnered with went to my log buyer and threatened him.

Told him if he kept allowing me to haul my logs, he was going to start harassing his employees and pulling over his lumber trucks—making it hard for him to operate.

The sheriff allowed his deputy to act this unprofessionally, just to destroy me.

That's how I got taken out—behind haters.

The charges the same lawman used to have me on the top ten most wanted list?

They were all dismissed.

What does that tell you?

The kingpin hater was behind all of this.

Just wanted everyone to know—when I said his death was a blessing, I wasn't trying to be mean. Just honest.

I'm sure after hearing all this, my readers can understand why I feel the way I do.

His death was a blessing.

It really and truly was.

Even God doesn't care for haters.

## ROOTS BY JOE ROACH

You can't get away with being a hater forever.

I'm proud to say I'm still here and more blessed than ever by a wonderful and great family. Jay, Larry, Jason, Jeremy, Wesley, Shane, Russell Jr., Ronnie, Ricky, Don, Bobby, Paul, Paul Jr., Dad, Ronnie Jr., Tommy, Ricky Jr., Jake—many more—I could go on and on. These are my family roots.

Roots I'm proud of and roots I hope never die because the Roach family are great and wonderful people. I love my family, my roots, and everything else about the Roach family there is to love and care about.

My daddy and all my uncles and cousins of the Roach family—I'm so blessed to have them. I want you all to know the Roach family comes from solid roots. That's how God blessed me—through my great family, the Roach family.

If your last name is Roach, Smith, or Krantz, you're family—either a cousin, aunt, or uncle. Which one doesn't matter because we're all family.

While I'm out riding around Straight Stone, I see a clear-cut from the side of the road as far back as I can see. I'm riding my black-on-black BMW convertible. It's mid-July, and I'm curious about this logging job. So, I put the top up before I start because the red dust is six inches deep, figuring I'll just stop by the car wash later.

I could see dust clouds a mile back from the equipment. When I finally made it back there, the road wasn't bad, but the dust was terrible. I should have known when I pulled up—it was one of Larry's jobs. All the machines were TigerCat machines.

After the loader operator finished chipping the trailer he had just started when I pulled up—maybe fifteen minutes—I heard the chipper throttle down, and then I saw my cousin Russell step out of the 234 TigerCat knuckle boom.

He walked over, and we shook hands and hugged. It had been a while since I'd seen him. He was operating one of Larry's jobs. I told him he shouldn't have stopped chipping on account of me.

He said he didn't stop because I pulled up. He stopped because he needed to switch trailers. That one was loaded. Puzzled, I asked, "Didn't you just put that trailer in as I pulled up?"

"Yeah," he said, "and it's already loaded with chips." He explained that from the time he throttles the chipper up to the time he throttles it back down—fifteen minutes—the chip trailer is loaded.

He had four skidders operating. Further back, it was swampy, so he had two TigerCat six-wheel skidders setting out skids for two 620E TigerCat skidders to take to the landing to maintain ground speed.

Putting out twenty-five loads a day and having to drag anywhere from half a mile to a mile, he had to depend on ground speed. All of Larry's jobs are about production. No matter what, it's got to go. Being a boss on Larry's jobs, you're never supposed to have any excuses because he makes sure you have the equipment needed to complete each day's goals and achievements successfully.

That's what's nice about being a boss on Larry's jobs—living stress-free. Just show up and let TigerCat do the rest. Russell chipped eight more loads in the two and a half hours I was there. He's a hard worker and dedicated. That again falls back to family roots. Russell is a great person.

I should send Larry a bill for the cost of detailing my black-on-black BMW. By the time I left there, it looked more like red-on-red. That red dirt and dust had found every crack, every seam to get in. Even the rubber around the trunk was coated with dirt and dust. That's what I get for taking a $40,000 car a mile off the road to be nosy. I should have known it'd be one of Larry's jobs.

That car means nothing. My family roots will always come before money. I'm glad I stopped that day. I need to get back around to see Russell again. I need to get back to riding around so I can see my family because one day, the ones I'm talking about now—and me—will only be remembered by memories and, of course, another headstone added to the Roach cemetery.

Sad but true, one day that's all it will be—headstones. If what they say is true, within seventy-five years of a person's death, they are forgotten, or to the living, they never existed. That's why I want all my family to know: If anyone knew love, it was us as far back as we can remember. Just remember, life is great, but Heaven is even greater and more beautiful than any life has ever been.

I've read the Bible from front to back. All of God's requirements have already been accomplished by us all, except for the kingpin HATER. He deserves everything he's got coming to him!

We have a great and wonderful God. He knows real, and He knows fake. Just remember, God doesn't say you need to go to church. All He wants from us is to believe in Him—one on one. He doesn't care—just believe. That's all He asks. He will never abandon us. That's a promise to everyone—except HATERS! God can't stand a HATER!

# Chapter 17

As I sit here on Christmas Day, 2024, I can't help but think about the many people in my family that I love and miss. It's hard to learn from mistakes if you continue to act as if nothing's your fault—something I found myself doing a lot back then. But now, I see that's gotten me nowhere.

I can see I need to change. All these great stories about my family and my family roots are true. I have always had a marvelous family to rely on. I don't mention my mama as much as I should. I'd like to say she's my mama—I loved her unconditionally like God intended me to. I didn't listen to what she said much. Daddy was the one I listened to the most. Still, when I got to be a teenager, that was very little.

When I was sixteen, I met an older lady. She was middle-aged, maybe forty years old. I wanted to leave home to shack up with her. Mama said no, but

Daddy said I could, so I left home. Daddy always said I had a job. Now and then, I'd show up, work a day, then take a month or two off.

My brothers and other family members that I've mentioned—they're the ones who stuck it out. That's why you never hear me take any credit. Daddy and my uncles spoiled me. I worked when I would, but really, I never had to. I've been spoiled from day one.

The first time I got whipped by my uncle, the others learned a lesson. I learned that if you could whip me, you could be my daddy too. You've read the stories about my family. It's true. I got my ass kicked a lot by certain cousins because they felt I was taking from them. Back then, I was. If my uncles were alive, I'd still be at fifty-four years old the same as I was at ten—still sitting at everybody's table because I was a son to them all.

They got a break for a few years when I ran off to shack up with Pat. Pat was the older lady's name. She told me when I left home to be with her that she would love and spoil me. I promised I would be as good as I knew to be. She kept her promise. She withdrew $100,000 from the bank.

Where the money came from, I don't know. Didn't care, didn't ask. She had it—that's all that mattered.

Pat knew my daddy. They were close to the same age. She knew my daddy was one hell of a man. She told me to my face—she made it no secret—she always wanted her some of my daddy. She always said he surely could, any time.

Pat believed in keeping it real, said whatever came to her mind. With that hundred grand, she could have slept with anybody she wanted—that would have been fine with me.

Back then, $100,000 was a lot of money to have on hand in a briefcase. That's why she doesn't believe a word the haters say about me being a thief. Never did I take a nickel from her that she didn't give me or spend on me in the three years we were together. I was more worried about being a hound dog than stealing. I had no reason to—she gave me anything I asked for.

Pat finished raising me from the time I was sixteen until I was nineteen. She taught me everything I'd need to know. She was my mama and everything else real mamas can't be!

She said I blessed her, but really, she blessed me. This was part of my journey through life that caused me to be spoiled even more. She paid for cars, trucks, and motorcycles. She helped spoil me—that's for sure.

I wanted to mention Pat in my book because she's a wonderful and marvelous person. I want to thank her for loving me and taking care of me the way she did!

I know she's still alive. She called my sister Jody last week to wish her a Merry Christmas and to check on me. Pat's seventy-five years old now. My sister said Pat told her the same thing about our daddy—at the age of seventy-five.

That tells me she's doing okay.

Just wanted to say I was blessed to meet her. Sure would be nice if we both could turn back time, but still, I wouldn't change a thing about me and her. She was a wonderful and great person.

She had enough heartache to last a lifetime. I'm not going to get deep into that, but I will say—just losing my son almost killed me. She lost two—her son and daughter.

She is a strong woman.

It won't be as long now as it has been. You raised wonderful kids—you will enjoy yourself when you get there.

We have a wonderful God. Your two kids will be there at the pearly white gates when you arrive.

FACTS.

I'm so glad I decided to learn about God. Because really, I had no clue.

If I'd said to certain people that I was going to heaven, they would have laughed and said, "Yeah right, Joe—stop playing."

That's happened before.

When that happens and you have no clue about God, you believe them. And as long as you leave it like that, in your heart and mind, that's what it's going to be.

When really—that's not how it is at all.

I'm glad I opened the Bible. Because if I hadn't, I'd have had no clue about what I know now.

Romans 4:5 – Him who justifies the ungodly. He makes those just that are unjust, forgives those who deserve to be punished, grants grace to those who don't deserve it.

Romans 3:10 – There is none righteous, not one.

Isaiah 64:6 – Jesus did not come looking for the righteous. He came looking for the unjust so He could make us just.

He is the only one who can justify the ungodly.

# ROOTS BY JOE ROACH

# Chapter 18

You can forgive a person who has harmed you, but that person has to be forgiven by you. No third party can forgive the person who harmed you but you.

As far as sin—all sins are against God.

Psalm 51:4 – David said, "Against you, against only you, I have sinned and done what's evil in your eyes."

Only God can forgive him because the sin committed was against God.

God is the only one who treats the ungodly as if they have always been godly. He is the only one who has the power to do so.

I learned from reading the Bible that no matter how guilty you are, if you come to God through Jesus

Christ, God will treat you as if you have never sinned.

Romans 8:33 – God is the only one who justifies.

God can dismiss all your sins.

God said, "Any sin shall be forgiven."

Matthew 12:31

Before I opened the Bible, even the ungodly judged me. I didn't know any different, so I believed them.

Why?

Because I had no clue about God. If they knew anything about God, they knew more than I did.

When they laugh at me now, I feel sad for them. They don't have a clue.

What made me open the Bible out of the blue?

I thought it was because I was curious. Now, I think it was God who made me curious.

When I didn't believe I could find peace, all I felt was condemned. Then He gave me peace by believing.

Once I believed, I knew I had been forgiven. Because I do have faith in God.

I'll never claim to be a 100% Godly person.

Even God Himself says it's not possible.

Ecclesiastes 7:20 – There isn't one man righteous on earth who never sins.

Even though you've been in church with God's people, you may need to try meeting Him one-on-one.

Just because you pray with your lips does not mean you have real love for God in your heart.

If you're living as a hypocrite—living an ungodly life—you're wasting your time.

Just remember—you are the kind Jesus came for.

He didn't come just for the godly. He came to justify the ungodly—like so many of us today.

We all need God now more than ever.

I read the Bible. I study the Bible. But still—to say I'm a godly person?

I can't say that.

But I can say—I'm a lot closer now than ever before.

I know I have a long way to go.

But at least now—when people judge me, they're judging me based on the person they want me to be.

They do that so they can make themselves look better. Feel better.

There are a lot of sad people in the world.

The saddest part?

They don't see it.

And they do it to themselves.

Going to church is not a requirement from God.

God says some churches have hypocrites—but not all.

A person who talks to God one-on-one doesn't need to ask a priest to forgive them.

Really—if a priest tells you he can forgive your sins, he's lying.

Only God can forgive your sins.

A priest can ask God to forgive you—but so can you.

You can do that one-on-one.

Just believe.

Talk to God. Let Him know you believe in Him.

He doesn't care if you don't know how to read or write. That has nothing to do with being a son of God.

Not knowing how to read makes it even easier.

Just sit back—and listen to your heart.

Because that's where you'll find God.

I'm more different than most white guys. The Black say I was the only white boy they knew who was born with a Black soul. My first sweetheart was a Black girl from up on the ridge. I don't have to say who—anybody that knew me, they knew who.

She was Black and beautiful—that's all that mattered. She's been my sweetheart since I first laid eyes on her. I'm fifty-four years old now. Her name is Kathy, and to this day, she's still my sweetheart.

That's when you know you have old-school love in your heart. That, along with a Black soul, I've been blessed my whole life—never took time to realize it until now. I'm fifty-four years old.

The first church I ever went to was a Black folks' church, but before I tell about going to church with the Black folk, let me tell the story from the beginning—the one that got me there.

I was at Bridgewater Plaza when this Black girl asked me about all my tattoos. I was covered from neck down—every part of my body marked with prison ink. She asked what I was drinking.

I said, "A Jamaican Lizard."

She asked if she could try it.

"Yes, you can try it. If you like it, I'll buy you one."

So she had a seat across from me at the table. She took a sip and said, "Yummy. Get you another, and I'll drink this one—if you don't mind?"

I got me another. We sat and talked. Her name was Tamika. She was from Callins, VA.

I asked, "How'd you get this far from home?"

It wasn't really that far—maybe an hour away.

"That's pretty far just to go out and hang," I said.

She was with a girlfriend who had a boyfriend living in Body Camp. He was one of the Fox boys. I'd known him and his family my whole life. When you're from around my way, it doesn't matter that you're Black—we're still family.

Tamika and I hooked up—as friends, dating, or whatever. Her girlfriend stayed with her boyfriend.

Tamika said, "I know a spot I think you'd like in Callins. Want to ride that far?"

By now, her friend Tarsia and David were sitting with us. David was a lifelong friend. We were best friends through grade school but hadn't seen each other in years until now. Strange how everything seems to work out.

Tamika and I walked to my car in the front parking lot. I hit the start button on my key. My black-on-black BMW convertible beeped, the lights flashed, the engine started.

Tamika said, "Is that your car?"

I said, "It is. Why?"

She said, "Well, really, Joe, I pictured you in a jacked-up truck—surely not a black-on-black BMW convertible."

I laughed. "I got a jacked-up truck if that’s what you’d rather ride in. We just gotta stop by my house and grab it."

Tamika shook her head. "No, the BMW is perfect."

We left Bridgewater, headed to Callins. When we got to the country roads in Callins, Tamika had me take a back dirt road.

# Chapter 19

About a mile down that gravel road, cars were parked along both sides.

She said, "Park here. We gotta walk just a ways up to the happening spot."

I've been to a lot of happening spots, but never one on the side of a dead-end dirt road like this. Most white guys wouldn't be here. But me? Black folk had been my family no matter where I was.

I parked. We walked up the dirt road. I could hear old-school blues being picked and sung, but I didn't see a house—just a tobacco barn beside the gravel road.

Tamika said, "This is it."

The place was pitch black outside. She opened the door. There I stood—the only white boy in a crowd of about fifty Black folk. Every single one of them stared at me like deer in headlights. Either I was crazy, or I was the police.

I was crazy, but never the police.

Tamika introduced me. That was all it took. I've been family with the Black folk in Callins ever since. I was twenty years old then. I'm fifty-four now, and still, I'm family to the Black folk in Callins.

The spot had a dirt floor, lit up by lanterns. The bar was made of old slab wood. Behind it, a man and an old Black lady sold beer from a cooler and shots of moonshine from a Mason jar. That old lady was cooking on a wood stove—just like my mama used to when I was growing up.

She fried chicken in one black skillet, fish in another.

These were the days I wish we could go back to—back when we wanted to be together, without all this nonsense.

That's where I met the Black folk preacher. He had stopped by for some of Mama's home cooking. That's what everyone called the old lady—Mama. Best food in the state. That's all I ever knew her by. She loved me. She always said I was her white son.

The preacher got himself a plate, took two shots of gut-burning moonshine, and said, "Okay, everyone, don't forget—Sunday service tomorrow. Plus, we're having a cookout. Mama's cooking. Black folk been fishing all week, preparing for this Sunday fish fry."

That's how I ended up at the Black folk church in Callins, VA—way back when.

I know every Black folk in six surrounding counties. They're all my family.

No white person has ever been around so many Black folk like Joe Roach. They are family, for real.

That Sunday service was great. I could tell God was in that church. When the choir started singing, it was like the life was sucked out of me—my whole body felt as light as a feather. I reached for the arm of my seat like I was about to float away.

I was twenty years old then. I'm fifty-four now. That's never happened again. Maybe I need to visit the Black folk church again. What you think?

People that use that "Niger" word have no clue what they're saying or what they're doing. The true meaning of "Niger" is an ignorant person. That's what they're doing—being ignorant.

God made us all perfect to Him.

We all know white folk who claim to be racist. It's not really about color. I'll leave it at that, 'cause this book is about good people and God. I'm not about to trick this book up with something we can't change.

How can people say who's not good when they know they're just as bad—if not worse? But that, you never hear.

All I ever hear is what's said about me.

I didn't care then. Now, I've learned what I didn't know back then. I'm stress-free. I don't care what anyone says, 'cause if you gotta judge me, you're hiding something about yourself.

It's true—Jesus came to save sinners. (1 Timothy 1:15) The law is to humble the self-righteous. The gospel is to help find yourself. Sinners are the only reason for the Bible's existence.

Only the Lord can clean you of your sins. Until you find God, you'll never see it.

You don't need anyone to guide you. I know a lot of elderly people who are very private—they're not about to talk to a preacher about their life.

I'm here to tell you, you don't have to. You can talk to God while riding down the road, sitting on your tractor. You can talk to God one-on-one at any time. He hears you.

A preacher is only there to guide you if you need it. But really, you don't need nobody but God.

So save yourself. Whoever else wants to be saved—they can do the same thing, the same way you did. Let's worry about you. Let them worry about them. You can't save them anyway. And it's really as easy as I said it was.

I don’t pray before every meal. Sometimes, I’m just hungry. I say thank you as I shovel it down. God knows your heart. You don’t have to constantly remind Him.

Or is it that you gotta constantly remind yourself?

Lighten up. Breathe a little. Live knowing it’s okay.

Here’s the edited version of your text, preserving the manuscript’s authentic voice while improving spelling, grammar, punctuation, and clarity. I’ve kept the original tone and style, ensuring readability without altering the natural flow.

---

Just know—if it wasn't for sin, we wouldn't know Jesus, our God. You’re going to sin every day, no matter what. FACTS—God said that.

(Mark 2:17) "It's not the healthy that need a doctor, it's the ones that are sick." Makes a lot of sense to me.

Faith is the chosen word. Why is that? We all understand what faith means—it means belief. In other terms, we might not understand, 'cause sometimes we don't understand God's way of meaning things. So faith is as simple as it gets. (Ephesians 2:8) "By grace, you have been saved through faith—not through love, not hope—but through faith."

---

# Chapter 20

If you've read this book, I'm sure by now you know—I'm trying to learn about God. God has reached out to me, given me the words to say, and helped me understand the things I write about in this book.

Even if you don't know God—just like I had no clue—listening to others, I thought I'd been abandoned a long time ago. But reading, learning, and seeing little things for what they really are, I know now—God has never abandoned me. If anything, I abandoned God.

FAITH is an understanding from the heart. (Romans 10:10) "With the heart, a person believes. Faith results in righteousness." Faith and love are related—like a brother, sister, mom & dad. That's real love, the kind that comes from the roots—where real love begins.

When you want to do good but can't—believe this, it's true. (Romans 7:18) "The will to do good is inside me, but actually being able to do it—I can't find it when I try."

(John 15:5) "Without me, you can do nothing."

If my phrases are not word-for-word, it's because I'm not looking at the book. What I write is how I remember and interpret it from the Bible. I've been reading and remembering a lot from the Bible for some time now.

I'm pretty slick when it comes to talking about the Bible—slicker than you'd think. So the next time you judge me, just know—you're wasting your time, 'cause I don't care what anyone thinks. I am who I am. I'll never be the one you can feed off of by making me look bad. Be careful what you say—I've seen things turn out bad for people like you—the ungodly, the ones who choose to stay that way.

I could go on and on, but this has to end. I like sharing my thoughts, my skills, what I learn, and how I think. Now, I know a lot more than I ever did about God.

I also like talking about my friends, my family, and my roots. My mama—I haven't talked about her much, but she is a wonderful, great person. I love her unconditionally—'cause she's my mama, and she deserves it.

I don't see her now. Her and Dad done got older. Back when I served my first ten years in prison, they were much younger—they came once a month. It was a five-hour drive from Smith Mountain Lake to Keen Mountain Prison.

I was in my late twenties and early thirties back then. Doing time then was nothing like it is now. Time changes everything—nothing stays the same. I was out almost twenty years. Now I'm fifty-four years old, back inside, doing ten more years.

This time, I’m not as far away as I was before. But now, Mom and Dad are up in age. I’d rather not see them than have them take a chance driving on these busy highways just to visit me.

Besides, if I’d never been around the kind of people I was around, I wouldn’t be in here in the first place. It’s my fault—100%.

Ain’t no reason to risk Mama and Dad’s lives coming to see me when all I had to do was listen to them and I wouldn’t be here. Daddy done told me time after time, "You keep layin’ with dogs, you not only gonna get up with fleas—you gonna get up with ticks, and worse—something you can’t get rid of—messin’ with those crack whores."

I’ve not been the smartest knife in the kitchen drawer. Must be why I’ve spent most of my life locked away. When I finish this ten, I’ll have done twenty-five years total.

I've written about it before—every time, it's never been my fault. At least, that's how I told it. Nothing was ever anything I did wrong—it was always someone else's fault.

But the truth is—I was arrested for murder. Convicted of receiving stolen property. Sentenced to ten years.

How is that possible?

I don't know—but it is. 'Cause I'm sitting at Bland Farm Prison, serving ten years, writing about my life's journey.

Some of my life falls under (Romans 7:18)—"I have it in me to do good, but how to actually perform doing good? I can't find a way to do it."

I'm here for a reason. God works in mysterious ways. Really, I can say—my life at the time was a rollercoaster without brakes, turned up to full throttle.

What God did—was a blessing. He saved my life.

The road I was on was a disaster waiting to happen. Full throttle, NOS bottle, no regulator—wide open. That was my lifestyle at the time. So you be the judge of what was about to happen.

Just being accused of murder was bad enough.

I see God's many blessings. I'm really not the kind of person people say I am. But still, they say I did it—because people love to gossip. That ain't good.

It's hard to defend myself while serving ten years for receiving stolen property. Everyone out there thinks I'm serving time for murder.

Hopefully, writing this book will help people see the real me.

I'm far from stupid. I can recite the Bible better than some folks who've been Christians their whole lives. Before three years ago, I never even opened a Bible. Everything I know, everything I talk about—I learned in three years. More than some learn in a lifetime.

I have an electrician degree. A masonry degree. And a college degree higher than a high school diploma. That's a lot more than some people have to show for twenty-five years of their life.

Now, I'm taking a computer class while I'm here at Bland Farm Prison.

People don't know the opportunities that exist in prison. Bland offers many different degrees—farming, agriculture, produce, loading dock, forklift training, and all kinds of safety training. No matter the job, they train you for it all. Then you get your license of certification.

If you want to better yourself and not come back, Bland is a good place to start. They offer a lot to help inmates. A degree can really help someone get a good job and stay out of prison.

I'm definitely taking advantage of everything they offer.
Here's the edited version of your text, preserving the manuscript's authentic voice while improving spelling, grammar, punctuation, and clarity while maintaining the original tone and style.

---

# Chapter 21

Today's timber harvesting has nothing in common with the way it was when my Daddy started his own logging business. What I remember about those first days, going with my Dad to his logging job when I was a boy, is that modern equipment today looks almost prehistoric compared to back then. Satellite views of property and cell phones were unheard of.

Very rarely did you hear of a clear-cut. Hardwood was always a select cut—if there was a clear-cut, it was pine.

We're talking back when Dad was logging with that winch tractor, bulldozer, and a front-end loader. Daddy worked like a mule the whole time me and my brother were young, growing up.

How my Daddy and uncles survived the dangers of logging back then—had to be God with them every step of the way. The old winch tractor Dad had didn't have a cab. It was like sitting on a death trap, with me and my brother hanging on to both fenders, winching trees, limbs falling, tree tops breaking. Now, as fast as things are going, you wouldn't last a whole day on one of today's logging jobs doing it the way they did back then.

I was glad to see my Daddy retire in good health. He built a successful logging business with the help of Jay, Larry, Jason, Jeremy, Rex, Hertford, and Roger. Dad had a lot of dedicated family members who were determined to see Papa Roach have a great life when he retired.

Him being in good health and having survived that long—after what me and my brother witnessed him going through—just to give us the best life he could while we were growing up, was a blessing.

It was a blessing to see him be able to do what he always said he'd do, if the good Lord was willing.

"All I'm gonna do is count my cows and farm."

I remember back in 1986 when the IRS came in. What they didn't take, they froze. Nothing coming in, nothing going out.

"Pay them $100,000, or take Mama and the kids and get out!"

Back then, Uncle Sam would put you out. Uncle Sam didn't care. He'd put you and your kids out in the street. Pay up or get out. That's how tax collectors were back then.

Daddy had maybe thirty head of cattle. He had to sell them. He sold his '66 Ford Fairlane—he loved that car. But he had to sell it.

After he got the IRS paid, that was a lesson well learned. That never happened again.

He had nothing left. His cows were sold. He had that winch tractor, bulldozer, front-end loader, and two log trucks. His brother Roger was with him the whole way.

That's how he started all over again—just him and Roger, helping each other. Then Ricky and Ronnie helped until they went out on their own. But Roger never abandoned Dad. Roger was a horse of a man. He raised his son, Rex, the same way—to be a hell of a man and forever be dedicated to Papa Roach.

That's what we call Dad.

'Cause to us, he's the kingpin—the man he's always been. His brother Roger was a great and wonderful uncle to me. Roger, like the others, was always good to me.

I remember my first beer. Roger got me and him one from Big Horn Market. It was a Saturday. We had just finished delivering a load of firewood. He stopped, gassed up the log truck. I was thirteen. He got me a pack of Marlboro cigarettes. Then he got me and him a forty-ounce Malt Duck beer each.

Roger Krantz was the greatest. He was solid.

He'd buy me cigarettes every day. I'd hide them in the truck.

Roger didn't smoke—he dipped snuff. I'd ride with him on every load. I know I was Roger's favorite—no doubt. He would freeze me to death riding with him in the winter. He didn't have to worry about getting me a forty, 'cause I was already frozen solid from him driving that '66 GMC log truck with the window down—his arm hanging out. What felt like below-zero degrees.

I asked, "Roger, can you roll the window up?"

He laughed as he rolled it up. "You not cold, are you?"

"No, Uncle Roger. I'm just froze as stiff as a board!" LOL

All I really said was, "Yeah, I'm cold."

Roger was the greatest.

I'll really be spoiled when I get to Heaven, 'cause I know without a doubt all my uncles are there. All my uncles were good to me.

I'm blessed to have—and have had—the family I have.

I'm so glad I got a better understanding about God.

Now, knowing what I know—that's FACTS—I know what a blessing it's gonna be when I get there. And I know all my uncles and my Daddy knew God in their hearts. To be as great as they were, they had to be blessed—with hearts as big as Texas.

I know that for a fact.

My family—they are great and wonderful people.

I'm not saying this just because they're my family. I'm saying it 'cause they were always good to me.

If you call me spoiled—my Daddy and my uncles done it.

I never really took the time to see how much people in my family cared about me. I was always wanting something. After I figured out all I had to do was ask, I was the most blessed kid in Roachtown.

Here's the edited version of your text, keeping the original voice and flow while improving spelling, grammar, punctuation, and clarity.

# Chapter 22

I read a lot about God—anything I see that's got to do with God and how other people feel about Him, I read it.

My Daddy, being set in his ways and the way he lives, the faith he's got—I'll never read anything that will come close to teaching me what my Daddy already knows about God's way. What came to him naturally, we can't learn by reading in a lifetime. God's way came through the roots when Daddy was born.

Daddy says, "Live right, do right, and righteousness—then you won't have to worry about nothing. Because it comes honest when you live right."

Being a good man, being an honest man—just the way my Daddy lives his life—God will always bless my Daddy. From the love I've felt, from the hearts I've been loved by growing up, God surely blessed us all. No matter what anyone says, they will never know the real heart of the Roach family the way God does.

The Roach love starts from the roots.

All my whippings growing up—now looking back—were blessings. Back then, I wished I was big. Now, I wish I was little again. Time changes everything.

I'm so happy to say, no matter what, the best thing that ever happened to me after getting locked up—God showed me what to look for. The man He showed me to be was the man my Daddy and my uncles have always been.

Just because they didn't go to church, that meant nothing. God looks at the heart—how a person lives and believes means more than any scripture he could ever read.

The Roach brothers—they all worked hard, asked nobody for nothing. They gave forevermore, never looking for anything in return. When my Daddy and my uncles did things for me—and for many others—they never said "You owe me." They thanked you and said, "Don't mention it."

They prospered in life, 'cause they lived right. You never saw my Daddy or any of my uncles with a handout. And if you did—you can bet they were the ones blessing someone else.

You can look at my Daddy and say he's blessed. He's the definition of a real man—the kind God will always bless, just as He did Job, after Job passed the test.

Look at what my Daddy and uncles survived—what they were put through to survive.

The things these eyes witnessed growing up—how life really was—most people wouldn't have a clue.

This I remember like it was yesterday.

Daddy was cutting timber for the Dallas family, just above their homeplace, down a long gravel driveway. Just before we got to the house, there was a field on the left. Daddy, our cousin Ricky, my brother, and I were there. Ricky worked for Daddy. Me and Jay were young—maybe nine or ten.

That morning, first thing, we followed Daddy into the woods. Daddy had the chainsaw. Me and Jay carried the gas and oil.

We got down in the woods, and Daddy cranked the saw.

It was a huge red oak—the first tree he was gonna cut. The oak was covered in thorns and briars, so he cut a path to get to it. Then he notched it—big notch—told us to stand back, up on the hill just a bit.

When he cut that oak, it fell just the way he had it notched to go.

It fell into another big ash tree. When it did, that ash tree bent over. The oak rolled. A big limb snapped from the oak. The ash tree sprang back up—slingshot that limb right toward Daddy.

Daddy—not looking back—was keeping an eye on that limb. He was trying to get away but found himself backed into that briar patch.

He couldn't get out of the way.

That limb hit him in the face, broke his nose, and knocked both front teeth clean out, onto the ground.

We ran to him, helped him find both his teeth. He put them in his shirt pocket.

He took a handkerchief, tied a knot in it, bit down on it—and finished out the day. That evening, he went to the dentist down on the lake.

Dentist Mr. Ashwell put both teeth back in his mouth.

That's how hard it hit him—to knock them out by the roots.

Men were made like this back then.

Daddy never went to a doctor. Never missed a day's work.

This was the man I saw struggle—to keep his roots planted.

Just because my Daddy can't read the Bible doesn't mean he's not a godly man.

In Daddy's heart—he's got God planted.

When I was a boy, the only God I knew was my Daddy.

That's how God wanted it.

Who better to teach me—than a man like my Daddy?

# Chapter 23

I don't think America will ever be as beautiful as it once was—way back when.

Back when we didn't have electric. When we didn't drink water from a bottle—we drank water from a pail, with a hand dipper. When water came from a spring that fed a stream—big enough to fill a small pond that overflowed.

Back when rain fell on that old tin roof—you could hear it as it overflowed the barrels beneath the ledge, filling them with rainwater—bathwater.

Back then, we thought we struggled.

Daddy said, "We didn't know struggles."

I never understood what he meant.

Now I do.

We got everything now that we didn't have back then—but now we struggle.

How crazy is that?

Daddy always said, "Be careful what you wish for, 'cause the grass ain't always greener on the other side of the hill."

Most people say, "Grass ain't greener on the other side of the fence."

Back then, we didn't need a fence. The mule never wandered far from the shack. Most of the time, it would be standing by the porch, waiting on someone to toss it an ear of corn.

When our sister Jenny was born, Daddy had a house built—a four-room house. We did have electric then, but still no water, no plumbing.

Every afternoon, if Daddy got in from work before dark, he'd grab the pickaxe and shovel—and he'd dig until dark.

Digging a hand-dug well.

How did Daddy and his brothers do all they did back then?

"But now we struggle."

After digging the well by hand, Daddy put plumbing throughout the house. Whenever another brother or sister was born, Daddy built another room onto the house.

That house grew—from a four-room house to a nine- or ten-room house.

Ended up being six of us—three boys, three girls. Eight total, with Mom and Dad.

People don't know struggles—like my Mom and Dad.

And still, if you ask them, they'll say they were forever blessed.

The hard times we remember seeing them go through, when we were kids?

They done forgot.

To hear them tell it—they find more good to think about than the bad they can't change.

I remember I was probably thirteen years old. My Daddy's best friend, the only person I ever saw my Daddy have around as a friend, was Wallace Tosh. He was married to my mom's sister, Debbie Tosh. They had five kids, two boys and three girls.

Wallace got killed in a car accident, leaving Debbie with five kids to raise. Not long after, Deb got sick.

She was in the hospital for months. Doctors didn't know what was wrong.

Mom and Dad had her five kids plus us, a total of eleven kids. Other family members were trying to get Mom and Dad to put Deb's kids in a foster home. Doctors had given up on Deb. They had no clue what was wrong. She was going to die.

Then they found out she had gastritis—that was the problem.

While she was in the hospital, Mom and Dad had to keep her kids in hiding because some people were trying to get child services to take them.

This went on for at least six months, until Deb recovered. She didn't get to see her kids 'cause Mom had to keep them in hiding. Child services was at the hospital waiting.

Mom and Dad, every morning before daylight, got us all together. We all went to Dad's job. We stayed there all day until dark before Mom could take us home.

Dad never believed in welfare. He fed all eleven of us. You'd never know all of us weren't his own kids. That's how much they loved us all.

If one got something, we all got it.

That's the kind of Mom and Dad we had. We know we were blessed way back when.

After about six months, Deb finally came home. That was the first time she got to see her kids since she got sick.

Mom and Dad could've turned them over to child services.

They said, we'll be damned if we ever do that.

My Mom and Dad have never so much as had a speeding ticket.

The only law they ever broke was making sure Deb's kids stayed together, after losing their Daddy and then, weeks later, almost losing their Mama.

Mom and Dad did what they had to do. They hid us all, kept us together, until Deb got well.

How many people do you think would do that now?

But now we struggle.

I don't understand.

It's been a blessing to revisit my past while writing this book.

It's also been a privilege to look back and still remember the many blessings we thought were struggles back then.

When Jesus was put on the cross, the Devil thought he had won. He thought he had conquered the world.

That was his plan all along.

But God turned the Devil's intentions into failure, into no hope left to hope for.

Jesus defeated sin.
Jesus defeated death.
He conquered a new life, eternal life.

That's the power God will show you through Jesus Christ.

Just as the Bible says, Jesus was crucified, then placed in a tomb.

The tomb was empty.

Jesus was gone.

Now, if you don’t believe in God, you’re a fool.

Remember, evil will never win.

Every breath we take, we borrow from God.

And he don’t owe us a thing.

# Chapter 24

We abuse God's justice. We abuse His love. A love more faithful than anything we will ever find on this earth.

No wonder we struggle, if that's what you wanna call it.

We've not really seen struggles, not like we're going to.

Now, that's a promise from God to all of us if we don't tighten up.

God can't keep doing this.

He's got to come back.

Because people have forgotten again, just like He said they would.

Time changes everything.

Even good into bad.

God's coming.

Are you ready?

If not, you will see struggles.

Amen.

# Chapter 25

My story, my roots, my life.

Everything you ever wanted to know, you'll read it right here.

This is the story no one else can tell except me.

## ROOTS BY JOE ROACH

My name is Joey Dwayne Roach.

I was born in Huddleston, VA, Bedford County, Smith Mountain Lake area.

I've always been a free spirit person.

I grew up not knowing God, or anything about God.

I didn't attend church or any Sunday service.

Though Mom and Dad didn't go to church, they showed us unconditional love.

They believed in God.

And the love we saw was more love than any Sunday service or church could give us.

We got God's love right there at home, on Sunday, from Mom and Dad.

Daddy was our God.

That's how God wanted it.

'Cause no man was greater than our Daddy.

And God liked that.

Because we were kids, and our Mom and Dad were wonderful parents.

There's one person in this world I hate.

Not even God can change the way I feel about Timmy.

When I was told by my sister Jody that he had died, I felt blessed.

Later, I told myself, that's not good to feel and think like that.

But my heart still feels nothing but hate for him.

Let me explain why.

What I'm about to tell you is nothing compared to how sick Timmy really was, but this one thing he said, I'll never forget it.

And I'm glad he's dead.

This is the reason I say what I say.

March 6, 2018.

My son, JJ, he was twenty years old.

He worked for my brother, Jay, at JTR Logging.

He stopped by my house that day.

I asked him to run out to the store to get me some gas.

He left.

He got killed on the way to the store.

They said he crossed the center line, head-on into a conversion van.

The next morning, Timmy stops by the gossip store in Huddleston.

He tells everyone I was arrested.

Said I had my son killed last night.

My cousin, who worked there, called me, trying to figure out what was going on.

I hate Timmy.

Not even God can change that.

That was my son.

Others may not care, but I do.

Because JJ was my son.

# Chapter 26

It's not godly to hate anyone. I hated him every day. I prayed for his death. That's one thing I know I got to ask God to forgive me for, the hate I have in my heart for Timmy. What I say is facts. So if you knew Timmy and didn't know he was that way, I just wanted the world to know—Timmy was not a good person at all.

I just wanted my readers to know why I hated Timmy. I'm sure now you all can understand why. I'm not a bad person for feeling the way I feel. What he done was uncalled for, and God made sure he paid for that.

Let's get back to writing about people that are worth our time, not people that ain't worth a dime.

All my uncles were great people. If their kids speak bad about me, it's because they mad at how good their daddy was to me. Cause I had no problem asking for anything I wanted. I always got what I asked for.

Really, it's only been a few haters in the Roach family. The kingpin hater just passed away in 2024. The other couple I never see, and that's a blessing I hope stays that way forever. They are the ones that say I'm the bad one of the Roach family. I'm sure you can tell after reading this book—that's far from the truth. That's really the only picture others want you to see, and really, there's not many bad ones at all in the Roach family. There are a few that ain't worth a damn. They are the ones that paint the picture of me being the bad guy. I'm more godly than most, they don't want people to see that. Facts. When I tell the truth, they can only hope it's a lie.

To know the ones that are haters—the kind of people that killed Jesus—you know when they start downing me, they got a lot of skeletons in their closet.

Believe nothing they say and only half of what you see. People have got really bad. It's sad when all that's left are haters. People would rather lie to bring you down than praise you with the truth. These are the kind of people we deal with every day. How much sadder can it get than this?

They've done it for so long, now this is what's normal. Lie, just to have someone to talk about. They don't care who it hurts—that's the pleasure they get out of lying and gossiping every day.

How much more can God take?

I know now the people I love, and me, myself, we ready. They might not know it, but they will when we get there. If I wouldn't have opened the Bible and cared about as many people as I really do, I wouldn't know myself what I know now. I can say proudly—we ready.

God said He came for us all, but first He was going to save the ungodly. Sounds crazy, but it's true. The godly He's not worried about—the ungodly are the ones He died for.

He makes the ungodly into godly. He forgives the ones that should be punished. He even forgives the ones that crucified Jesus. He gives blessings to the ones that do not deserve it.

Do you think Jesus was sent for only the good?

Jesus was sent to change the bad, then take us all as good back with Him. Good is good, but bad can be made good through Jesus Christ.

Mark 2:17—When Jesus heard, He said, "They that are just have no need of a physician, but the ones who are sick. I came not for the godly but for the ungodly to repentance."

That's my understanding of what God said.

For God to change my heart and continue to bless me, even after some of the mad and hateful things I said—God doesn't listen to what comes from my lips. God listens to what comes from the heart.

Jesus told me to write that, so I did, because it's the truth.

I've never not believed in God, but I lived ungodly. I'll be the first to admit that. I think sometimes you can mislead yourself from God's blessings and favor. The Devil will trick you, so you continue doing ungodly.

Life is made up of many tricks you might think are blessings, but the whole time, it's the Devil's work. Sometimes when they say, "it's too good to be true"—that's a real and true statement.

As long as I was rewarded, I didn't care whether it was good or bad. That's really the reason I've spent the biggest part of my life in prison. What's sad is that I didn't see it until twenty-five years had been wasted.

Before I opened the Bible, I fit the description of being ungodly. But now, I still look the same. My appearance hasn't changed in person, but my attitude and my heart have changed—great and gracefully.

When God comes into your life, He leaves peacefully, so you know He’s always with you. That’s God’s greatest gift.

If anyone ever needed God to be a part of their life, it was me—Joey Dwayne Roach.

I don’t deserve to be justified, but God will justify me anyway, as if I've never been unjust.

For the Son of God has come to find and save them that was lost. Luke 19:10.

# Chapter 27

Revisiting my life through my thoughts and memories, I see many blessings now that I never saw before. It's amazing how a person's demeanor changes when God is in their life.

Just like me.

A lot of people in prison—I sit and watch them stress, either about doing time or about a woman.

That's one thing I'm so glad about—I'm stress-free.

I've never really stressed about doing time or about a woman during any time I've had to serve. I think women are wonderful, great, and beautiful, but to stress over one—surely not me. I'll be good to all women, but when I'm doing time, just let me do me. I like doing time stress-free.

The past three years since I been reading the Bible, plus a lot of different Christian books floating around in the dayroom library, I've had plenty of books to help me learn about God.

As you know, I do not ask these inmates—better known as haters—nothing. If you can't send them a Cash App for dope, they don't have time for you. So I'm glad not to have any dealings with them.

I like my job. I actually want to better myself.

After work and schooling each day, I'm ready to kick back in my cell, relax, and read about Jesus. That really helps me continue to stay stress-free. That's what I'm doing right now—January 12, 2025—writing in this book about my roots.

One thing I have figured out—as long as I'm in my cell writing in my book, I'm not getting in trouble. No matter where a person is in this world, they can always find the Devil. That spells trouble.

I seem to get blamed for everything, no matter what.

I've always been labeled as a master manipulator, a master in corrupting others into getting what I want. I deny doing anything like that. So as long as I'm in my cell, I can say it wasn't me.

This time, I like where I am. I've been charge-free for four years. I'm not into anything like I was when I served my first ten years.

Back then, yes, I was a wizard in manipulating. But now, I'm just trying to do my time, mind my business, and learn about God.

Now I know—God can save me. But He can't give me back what I lost from being a fool.

Time stops for no one.

Earth is where we are. Heaven is our destination.

When I get home, I want to love my family and water my roots. I've put them through a lot. My roots must be solid because I'm blessed with a wonderful family.

I'm happy no matter where I'm at because God will always be with me.

Amen. The End.

# ROOTS BY JOE ROACH

www.ingramcontent.com/pod-product-compliance
Lightning Source LLC
Chambersburg PA
CBHW070750180626
46818CB00007B/3061
* 9 7 8 1 6 3 7 5 1 5 2 4 2 *